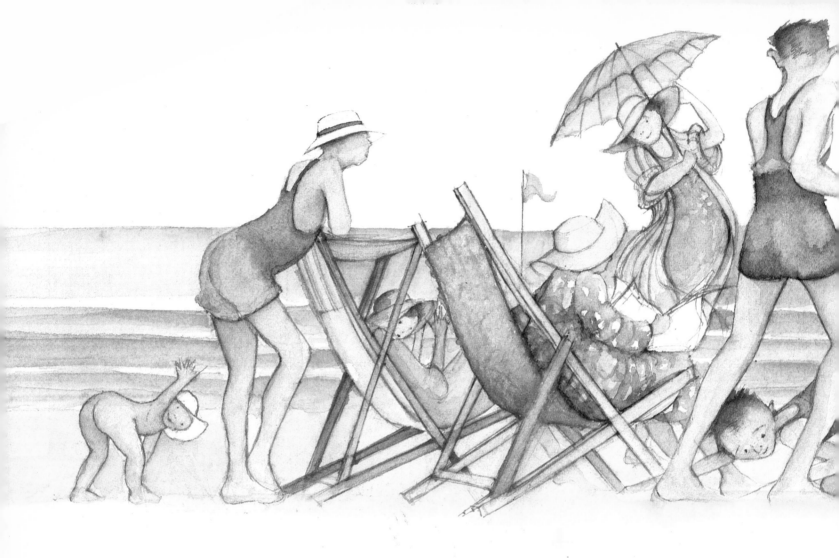

OTHER BOOKS FROM KANE/MILLER

One Woolly Wombat
The Magic Bubble Trip
The House From Morning to Night
Wilfrid Gordon McDonald Partridge
Brush
I Want My Potty
Girl From the Snow Country
Cat In Search of a Friend
The Truffle Hunter
Goodbye Rune
Winnie the Witch
The Umbrella Thief
The Park Bench
Paul and Sebastian
Sorry, Miss Folio!
The Night of the Stars

The Tram
to
Bondi Beach

Elizabeth Hathorn

Illustrated by Julie Vivas

A CRANKY NELL BOOK

KM Kane/Miller Book Publishers

Brooklyn, New York & La Jolla, California

For Keiran and Saxon
and especially for
my father
who knows about trams
and paper boys

First American Edition 1989 by Kane/Miller Book Publishers
Brooklyn, N.Y. & La Jolla, California

First Published in Australia in 1981 by Methuen Australia
(A division of Octopus Publishing Group Australia Pty Ltd)

Text Copyright © Elizabeth Hathorn 1981
Illustrations Copyright © Julie Vivas 1981

All rights reserved. For information contact:

Kane/Miller Book Publishers
P.O. Box 529, Brooklyn, N.Y. 11231-0005

Printed and bound in Italy by New Interlitho S.P.A. Milan
1 2 3 4 5 6 7 8 9 10

Library of Congress Cataloging-in-Publication Data

Hathorn, Elizabeth.
  The tram to Bondi Beach / Elizabeth Hathorn ; illustrated by Julie
Vivas
      p.   cm.
  Summary: Keiran longs to be a paper boy and sell papers to the
passengers on the tram that goes by his flat in a small Australian
town.
ISBN 0-916291-20-0
[1. Street-railroads—Fiction.   2. Newspaper carriers—Fiction.
3. Australia—Fiction.]   I. Vivas, Julie, 1947-   ill.   II. Title.
PZ7.H2843Tr   1989
[E]—dc19   88-31931
                                              CIP
                                              AC

Keiran O'Grady loved the trams that rattled past his apartment at Bondi. He loved the strange gnashing sound of the wheels on the silver rails.

Each morning he and his little sister Isabelle would watch through their window as the trams crisscrossed in front of them, laden with people on their way to work.

Keiran would often walk with his father to the tram to wave good-bye to him. Sometimes the early morning tram was so crowded it was hard to believe his father could ever fit into it. But Dad would put his foot up on the running-board, and then, with his hands firmly on the curved brass rail, heave himself mightily forward.

Passengers would edge back a little, and then just a little more, and Dad would be on and away. He always waved good-bye to Keiran with his folded newspaper.

Dad always bought the morning and evening paper from Saxon, the tall blond boy from Francis's news agency. Keiran loved to watch Saxon swing along the running-board of the tram while it was at the stop, like an agile monkey selling his papers quickly before the tram began to move.

He wanted to be a paper boy just like Saxon, but Dad said he was too young.

Sometimes in the summer Mom and Dad would take Keiran and Isabelle for a swim at Bondi Beach. It was only a few tram stops away, but Keiran loved every minute of the ride. He would sit up so proudly on the slatted wooden seats in the open car, wind blowing through his hair.

He loved to peer out for that first glimpse of blueness as they rounded the corner to Bondi Beach and everyone jumped up wanting to be first on the running-board, first off the tram and first onto the soft yellow sand.

Keiran had asked his parents so often about being a paper boy that on his ninth birthday Dad spoke to Mr. Francis about it.

"Yes, I believe I could do with another boy for the rush hour," said Mr. Francis. "Saxon can watch out for him, and if he's any good I'll take him on permanently."

Keiran felt important standing on the windy corner next to Saxon with a bundle of papers under his arm and a fat money purse on a belt around his waist. But Saxon wasn't pleased at all. Saxon didn't talk to him, except for the first night when he said angrily, "This is my job here! It's for someone tough and quick—not small fry like you. And this tram stop's my territory! You just stay put and leave me to do the trams, see. Just don't bother me."

Keiran said nothing. He just stayed in one spot selling his papers to the hurrying passengers that leaped down from the tram. He watched Saxon with envy as he jumped up on the running-board swinging so quickly from door to door just like a conductor.

Saxon flicked the newspaper expertly from under his arm, and, at the same time, juggled the change with the same hand. He was so quick that he could almost get along the entire length of the tram before the bell rang and it took off from the stop.

This only left a few papers for Keiran to sell.

Keiran was determined to join Saxon on the running-board of the tram and be a proper paper boy. But he was afraid to do it. Afraid he would be slow; afraid he wouldn't be able to balance himself and to reach into his money purse quickly enough.

At home he practiced flicking a newspaper from under his arm, folding it in two with one movement, and cupping his hand to receive the imaginary change. Finally he knew he could do it with one hand and swing along the railings with the other. He was ready to show Saxon that small fry could do it!

The night he decided to sell his papers from the running-board it was raining lightly.

When the tram rolled into the stop, he leaped up eagerly ahead of Saxon. He thrust his face in at every door crying out, "Paper!" Money was pressed into his fist. Papers were flicked—six, seven, eight—from under his arm.

He swung to the last car as the tram shuddered slowly forward. He had to find change. His hand fumbled around the money purse feeling for the familiar coin. He couldn't find it. He looked down. When he finally pressed the coin and the paper into the waiting hand, the tram had already begun picking up speed.

He couldn't jump now with the ground spinning by him. He thought of Saxon's cold stare. He had to do it. Now, now, before it was too late, before it was impossible.

He held his breath in fear as he jumped onto the wet pavement. He might have stayed on his feet if he hadn't landed so heavily with the bundle of papers to one side.

But his feet went from under him, and the papers flew out of the strap and scattered in muddy puddles as Keiran rolled over and over and then stopped.

The conductor was calling angrily, though relieved to see that the boy was all right as he climbed to his feet. Keiran was glad when the familiar "ding, ding" sounded again and the tram rolled on, taking away those staring passengers along with the angry conductor.

Suddenly Saxon swept past him picking up the scattered papers and stacking them with whirlwind movements.

"Don't worry, Keiran. You've only messed up a few papers—the rest are all right," he said awkwardly. "Are you O.K.?"

Keiran was so glad at Saxon's sudden friendliness that he forgot his sore knee and elbow for the moment. But Dad had jumped off the tram and he was furious.

"That's it, Keiran," he yelled. "That's the end of your paper boy's job. I never dreamed you'd be so silly as to jump off a fast moving tram. Never."

Before Keiran could speak, Saxon came to the rescue once more.

"He's never done it before, Sir, and he won't do it again—will you kid? Give him another chance. He's a great paper boy. Quick at selling papers and quick with change too. Just one more chance."

Dad walked silently with Keiran and Saxon to Francis's newsstand. Keiran was afraid he'd lost his job as a paper boy forever.

"I don't want my boy leaping from moving trams," Dad told Mr. Francis firmly.

Mr. Francis looked down at Keiran's miserable face.

"Well, I don't know . . .," he said slowly. "Of course, there is that job coming up next week down at the beach. Do you think you could handle that? It's on the corner just two stops down; you'd have to carry a heavy pile of papers."

"That's O.K., Mr. Francis," Keiran said eagerly.

"*And* ride in the tram to get there."

"Oh, yes, Mr. Francis."

"*And* pay your own fare."

Dad seemed quite happy about the new job at the beach as long as Keiran rode *inside* the tram and not on the running-board.

So every night Keiran and Saxon walked to the stop together carrying their papers. Keiran would catch the first tram to the beach. It was always busy there and when he'd sold all the papers, he'd catch the tram back.

Those tram rides were the best part of the job for Keiran. He just loved the sound and the smell and the swaying movement of the trams as they spun along the silver rails.

It was wonderful being a paper boy and having a friend like Saxon Francis who was a paper boy too.

But Keiran knew that when he grew up he wouldn't sell papers anymore or even be a conductor swinging along the running-board.

He'd be the driver, taking those trams careening, rattling, flying—down the hill to Bondi Beach.